CLIMATE CHANGE
APOCALYPSE

A young Engineer's travels into the science
and politics behind global warming

STUART GRIFFITH

To order additional copies of this book, contact:
Xlibris
844-714-8691
www.Xlibris.com
Orders@Xlibris.com

ISBN: Softcover   978-1-6698-1949-3
         Hardcover   978-1-6698-1950-9
         EBook   978-1-6698-1948-6
Library of Congress Control Number: 2022906600
Print information available on the last page

Rev. date: 04/07/2022

To
Lucero

CONTENTS

ACKNOWLEDGEMENTS

With appreciation and thanks
to good friend and fellow author
Price Schwenck

Also
for the help and support
received from
Josh Fraser
Veronica Maybury
Elinor Griffith
Olga Collazo
Mary Flores

And with special mention for
Dr. John F. Griffith
whose encouragement and good advice
as always proved invaluable.

PROLOGUE

The early part of this twenty-first century has seen the rise of a very active and vocal environmental movement. Its influence has spread from universities into our very social and business structures. The belief that humankind is influencing and even causing climate change through the use of fossil fuels has become mainstream thinking. It is no longer unsettled science but well established and beyond doubt. Indeed, the 2015 Paris Climate Accord holds that the present warming trend could cause as much as a 7°F (4°C) increase over preindustrial times by the end of this century and potentially cause chaotic destruction to our planet and way of life. This has translated into a new narrative by alarmists that climate change is the existential threat of our times and drastic action must immediately be taken to mitigate this temperature rise. The movements driving this message now extend to the highest levels of government, business, and academia and are orchestrated by a well-financed environmental movement.

It is also noteworthy how proponents for and against this climate activism tend to break down ideologically, with liberal left-leaning proponents supporting it and skeptics of this new religion tending to be on the conservative right politically.

The story that follows traces the experiences of a young engineer trained in the environmental sciences as he progresses in his career with a multinational oil company and confronts the realities of climate change.

CHAPTER I

A Foundation for Environmentalism

In May 2015, a big day in my life was unfolding. I, Scott Paladino, was about to graduate from engineering school with a master's in climatology. My graduating class was assembled in the large student union hall at Polytechnic Business and Science University on the outskirts of Boston and just waiting for graduating proceedings to get underway. There was lots of buzz and excitement among the throngs of students and parents.

Engineering school had been a big challenge all the way, not made any easier by my decision to play varsity hockey. Both endeavors in different ways were very rewarding, and I had no regrets even though it sometimes seemed there were just not enough hours in the day. But there I was, alongside my good friend Jim McNamara, both of us kind of sighing with relief that the long days of studying were behind us. We were both from the Midwest, and it turned out that neither of us was able to have our parents here for the big event. But that was OK. My dad was an engineer and had administrative responsibilities in the local municipal utility, and travel was just out of the question at that time.

Anyway, proceedings finally got underway, and Jim and I finally received our master's-level diplomas with a strong sense of accomplishment. But we could not resist some back-and-forth banter as to how much they were worth. Jim would be working with a large environmental foundation, and I was on my way to Houston, where I would be working for a major oil company.

The featured speaker for this graduation ceremony was Dr. Leroy Lando, recognized as one of the foremost scientists in climatology and a member of the National Oceanic and Atmospheric Association. He was to address the subject of climate change and its growing importance in our lives. We were obviously very interested to hear what he had to say.

It didn't take long to see where he was going. After the usual aphorisms about climate change and its existence over many millions of years, he then directed his comments to the growing levels of carbon gases affecting global warming. He was quite adamant that because the UN'S very prestigious Intergovernmental Panel on Climate Change (IPCC), representing many distinguished scientists using their various computer models, had concluded the science was so, it must be so. Any doubt or skepticism was just a denial of the science. To my amazement, he started getting quite emotional, accusing nonbelievers in this science to be deniers and even infidels. "The future of our planet is at stake!" he exclaimed.

Jim had a look of surprise. We were both trying to understand the speaker's line of reasoning. Isn't science always about hypothesizing and being skeptical? Where was he going? It soon became obvious: "Fossil fuels and the oil companies who supply them are the culprits. The oil companies are no different from the tobacco companies back in the 1980s. Their products can, and must, be replaced by renewable fuels such as solar and wind." Jim and I found this interesting because our just-concluded studies had clearly shown this was not possible for economic and technical reasons, and that would be the case well into the future.

We both lapsed into "watch gazing." How much longer was this esteemed scholar going to go on? Mercifully, the speech did come to a close. Quite clearly, our classroom studies hadn't covered some challenges that lay ahead. Yet, at the same time, the good professor's remarks did trigger some fresh thoughts about my real beliefs and understandings about the subject of climate change.

Our university curriculum on environmental studies was obviously based on today's best-known science on climate and what causes it to change. That covered many aspects of the subject, from prehistoric times and the heating and cooling periods right up to the pre– and post–Industrial Revolution periods.

We had learned that climate changes have always been a feature of our planet and have significantly affected how plants, animals, and more recently, Homo sapiens, have lived. The temperature trend since the mid nineteenth-century premodern Industrial Age has been pretty specific since modern scientific measurement methods became available. That trend monitored a slow warming, which continued for most of the twentieth century, but then the trend line actually flattened by the end of the 1990s. This plateauing or flatlining of the trend line appears to have continued into the twenty-first century's first two decades. Apparently, this is challenged by climate activists who explain this as being a pause, an aberration, and the warming trend will soon continue its upward trajectory.

Our many classroom studies were replete with seminars, visiting experts, and ever so many hours working with the highly technical algorithms that directed our work with the supercomputer models. These models purported to show the road ahead for global warming and climate change, but constantly changed as our basic assumptions and inputs changed. However, they seemed to bring some order and discipline into the study of climate and temperature change, and our professors appeared to be OK with that. And of course, there were the UN IPCC reports and forecasts that were central to this thinking and gave this "science" the necessary credibility.

Their overall conclusion, which our own studies tended to corroborate, was that, in spite of the pause, the temperature trend would continue upward overall, and the computer models confirmed this. Planet Earth would heat between 4 and 7°F (2–4°C) by 2100. These differentials were versus a baseline of the preindustrial 1860s. Allegedly, this warming would have a catastrophic impact on human life as we know it; agriculture would dry up, causing millions to perish, glaciers to melt, and oceans to rise; submerging communities; et cetera, et cetera. One of our professors referred to this as the *Armageddon scenario*.

I had always felt, in spite of all the hyperbole, that maybe there were too many subjective assumptions and variables in this calculation, and therefore, it would need further examination. But then, who was I to question this "settled science" that the very mandarins of climate science had blessed?

CHAPTER II

From Campus to the Real World

Houston, Texas, has an impressive skyline, with its many high-rise office buildings. And none is more impressive than the fifty-six-story APEXEnergy building, head office of my new employer. But then Houston is the unquestioned oil capital of the world, a world that seemed destined for some major changes in the years ahead. Attacks on the fossil fuel industry and its future were already in the news. I couldn't help reflecting on this and that indeed, I was heading into a world that would be challenged by just that: change!

It was May 15, 2015, and I was reporting for my first day of work. I would report to Nigel Brown, assistant manager, for downstream training on the forty-second floor. As I got off the elevator, it was apparent that I was not the only one reporting for work at APEX on this day. There seemed to be about fifteen or twenty others who were in my age range and, like myself, fresh off university campuses.

Nigel was waiting for us in the reception area, and after introductions, he led us to a large conference room. In front of each seat, a folder was placed, neatly identified with each individual's name and containing literature on the company and a lot of standard employee forms, which would enroll us officially.

Nigel then proceeded with a PowerPoint presentation, which he described as an orientation session for new employees joining the APEXEnergy organization. It started with a broad overview of the hydrocarbon industry, the so-called Big Oil industry, and its significance in the broader energy industry. He highlighted energy trends and the roles of different sectors going back decades and projecting forward to 2040 and beyond. Interestingly, the hydrocarbon mix of oil, natural gas, and coal (that is, fossil fuels) would continue to dominate in world energy demand by up to 80 percent in 2040. This implied a huge increase in fossil fuel demand since world economies and energy demands would be significantly larger by midcentury. The other 20 percent would include nuclear, hydro, and other alternative developing forms of energy. The still-developing world in parts of Asia, Indochina, and especially the African continent would depend on fossil fuels for a long time into the future.

I kept waiting for some comments on the new green revolution, which we were hearing more and more about. What was the role of renewable energy in this mix? Was not the transition to solar, wind, and biomass energy to be a big part of this future?

The answers finally showed up on the charts. It was estimated that less than 7 percent of the world's energy would derive from these sources by 2040. Advanced economies such as North America and Europe would lead the way with 17 percent and 15 percent, respectively, estimated. Japan, South Korea, and Australia would be in the same bracket. The developing world would still remain heavily dependent on the logistical cost and efficiency of coal and petroleum to fuel their economies and raise their living standards. Still, all these projections were somewhat surprising in view of the major commitment of resources and publicity focused on a transition from fossil fuels.

If this analysis with data sourced from the International Energy Agency (IEA) was even close to correct, the oil business and the coal industry were going to be around for a very long time, even as they evolved to new realities.

Then Brown switched gears. "You all might be asking at this point, 'Who is APEXEnergy, and how does this company fit into this big-picture world of energy?'"

APEXEnergy had been a little-known Texas oil-drilling company back in the early twentieth century that became successful in the rich Texas Permian Basin, and through successive acquisitions became a major force in the industry by the 1940s. From a base of successful exploration and production, it expanded into refining and marketing, first in the Midwest and then nationally. Post–World War II saw massive growth in the economy and, with it, demand for petroleum products. From its strong domestic base, APEXEnergy further grew its exploration and production internationally with operations in the Middle East and Latin America. This was followed by still further downstream acquisitions.

Today, the APEXEnergy flag is a familiar sight in 165 countries, and APEX has become one of the five largest private oil companies in the world. At the same time, it has become much more than just a Big Oil company. Byproducts from basic oil refining have given rise to a large petrochemical division, which produces the basic raw materials for the manufacture of plastics and even the synthetic fibers that feed the garment industry. Perhaps a good percentage of the clothes we all were wearing today were because of this industry and maybe even this company!

I could not help wondering how much society at large knew or understood this.

And then there was yet another level: the little-publicized but world-class research and engineering department, employing literally thousands of engineers and scientists dedicated to fundamental research and development in many energy-related fields, such as new battery technology, hybrid and electric car development, new materials, and even alternative energy such as biofuels, to mention a few of its activities.

The energy industry involved a lot more than the familiar pump at the corner service station!

CHAPTER III

·············· ❖ ··············

Getting to Know the World of Big Oil

The department of Environmental Affairs, where I would be working, was a unit organizationally within the Public Affairs department. Jim Lavignon was the general manager of this Environmental group, and as an environmental specialist, I would report to him. He appeared to be a genial fellow—in his mid forties, I guessed—with an engineering background. He had been in environmental management with a major chemical company. Those guys knew all about the safety and environmental hazards of handling toxic materials, so APEXEnergy had hired him away some five years earlier. It seemed he had proven to be a valuable player on teams handling oil spills and cleanup operations. Although these events were infrequent, they were an ever-present risk in the oil industry. I also guessed that his personality made him a good communicator in the public relations forum.

Our first meeting involved his explaining the scope and importance of environmental management within the APEX corporation and slanted, understandably, toward the activities I would be involved in. Those pretty much came down to monitoring what outside activist groups were up to and preparing position papers for use by public relations and operating management in their outside communications. This was a long way from engineering school, but as my old pal Jim McNamara would say, "Hey, you gotta start somewhere."

We had some discussion about the company mission statement on the environment, but this seemed—at least to my inexperienced understanding—imprecise and probably a work in progress.

Jim then emphasized that for the months ahead, I would be in a training and development program. I had to become intimately familiar with all the company operations, and this would even involve working on assignments in various departments. This sounded interesting and like something I had hoped for. I was to begin this training program the following week.

This meant time and actual work assignments in upstream Exploration and Production as well as in the so-called downstream departments, Refining and Marketing. These common industry designations covered the departments and their activities, from finding crude oil to transporting it, refining it into finished products, and marketing it to the consuming public.

The technology and pure complexity in each of these areas were impressive, and my limited exposure would hardly scratch the knowledge's surface. But this orientation, in addition to giving me some understanding of the processes at work to make and market petroleum products, would provide me with the contacts I might need in the future to resolve problems related to these areas.

Another major area was the Petrochemical division, which was basically a company within the company and a major profit center for APEXEnergy. The nearby APEX refinery usually supplied the naphtha feedstocks for the chemical-processing units. The processes were totally integrated. Earlier presentations had already brought out the fact that these Petrochem products included the raw materials for the plastic and synthetic fiber industries, essential materials for our way of life.

Do the critics of this industry have any idea how complex and crucial this hydrocarbon industry is to their way of life?

During the next few months, I also learned that while most of our personnel, and many engineers I talked to, saw environmentalism as important and something to take seriously, it was not a high priority in daily operations. They were very busy just running the business. As one department manager expressed, "We are all committed to clean air and water, and we have actionable programs in these areas. The broader question of CO_2 emissions from fossil fuels and their effect on global warming has very thin, if any, scientific support."

This point of view was fairly common, and since he had a technical background, I respected his opinion.

The months of training soon stretched into a year and beyond before I was back with Lavignon, working on focused environmental issues. There was increasing noise about the "Green New Deal" coming from politicians and the media. A faction of the political left was suggesting that we should "greenwash" everything from car and airplane transportation right down to building remodeling and even domestic housing, all toward mitigating heat-causing emissions produced by man's use of fossil fuels. The proposals for accomplishing this were so bizarre that the majority of the public, to the extent that they were even paying attention, would just shake their heads in disbelief. And yet, as foolish as this narrative seemed, the media appeared to be a willing accomplice and even gave it some credibility. This green thinking had already extended to the oil industry, where companies such as APEXEnergy were being urged to take on a lower profile in the hydrocarbon business and actually promote a transition to alternate energy. It appeared some of our competitors were actually embracing these ideas. Whether this was just a matter of virtue signaling or a reality remained to be seen.

As time went by, Lavignon seemed to be testing me and asking for my opinions on more and more. This was all purpose driven, and as a result of it, I found myself digging ever deeper into the science and technical issues surrounding climate change and its many controversies. This had become anything but a settled science. Many scientists had shifted from so-called believers to skeptics and even deniers. The literature was replete with competing theories.

This whole debate had a rather disturbing dimension to it, at least in my way of thinking. Evidence was mounting that the debate had split pretty much along political lines, with the Democratic left advocating against fossil fuels and indeed the industry and its role in and even responsibility for global warming, and the conservative right challenging this assumption.

Since when had science become a hostage to politics? It seems when politicians see potential for political gain.

Considering the ideologies involved here, the answers required much deeper analysis.

Then one day, Lavignon advised me that the two of us would be going to Europe and we had to leave immediately. Climate activists were on the move against APEXEnergy operations in the UK.

CHAPTER IV

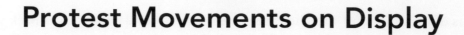

Protest Movements on Display

The activists were mounting protests against the petroleum industry in different markets and ominously had selected APEXEnergy as a special target. We were headed to the APEXEnergy offices in London, where some of our retail service station operations had been brought to a standstill as organized protests were blocking entrances. Our briefing paper included the familiar and usual background data, including that activists were targeting oil companies for being responsible for so-called CO_2 pollution and that the activists would use APEXEnergy, a major player in the industry, as an example.

The press and media also alleged that APEXEnergy and the industry as a whole were not doing enough to mitigate the effects of fossil fuel consumption and help phase to renewable energy sources. Moreover, the oil companies had known and kept secret for years the fact that CO_2 emissions from use of their products were greenhouse gases and therefore, ultimately, these same companies were responsible for man-made global warming. Climate change–friendly Europe had become a focal point of this aggressive attack on our industry, and as mentioned, we were to be the trial run for similar actions elsewhere.

Upon our early morning arrival at Heathrow Airport, Lavignon and I were met by an APEXEnergy UK representative who drove us directly to APEX headquarters in Central London. In advance, we had scheduled a 10:00 a.m. meeting with senior UK management. The proceedings began with an update on events throughout the previous day and nighttime hours, complete with video coverage.

Mobs of protesters had essentially shut down eight London-area service stations. The main loading rack for fuel-product trucks adjacent to our refinery had also been essentially shut down by a blockade at the main gate. In all instances, the police had attempted to maintain accesses but were only partially successful. Local TV news stations were out in force and holding on-site interviews with seemingly anyone willing to talk to them. Some protesters self-identified as being from the Sierra Club, the World Earth Council, and the Green Party, and of course, numerous placard-carrying individuals just seemed anxious to see themselves on TV. All had the same messages about saving the planet : bad oil companies being the CO_2 culprits, facing Armageddon in fifteen years, and on and on. Their statements and the chaotic scenes seemed to be well edited for messaging on the nightly news. The intended perception was accomplished, that being fossil fuels posed existential threats to the environment.

One intrepid reporter dared to ask, "If there were no gasoline and heating oil, how would our society continue to exist?"

The loud response was replete with vulgar insults, thinly veiled for media consumption. So much for any rational dialogue. Surely, these mobs with their megaphones were the minority and did not represent civilized society as a whole. Apparently, the media outlets didn't think so.

For days, the company had been besieged with requests to comment on these developments and had done so. But the volume seemed to be only increasing, and clearly, more directed statements, plus some targeted interviews, would have to occur. Lavignon and I were asked to help with this, so I could see we were not going home for a few days.

The meeting moved on to evaluation of the boycott threat to APEX business operations. In addition to the overall bad public relations campaign for the APEX brand, the more immediate practical concern was the shutdown taking place at our service stations, which in turn was affecting our refinery operations.

This was hurting the cash flow of not only our company but also our independent service station dealers and their employees.

Where was this going, and what, if anything, could be done about it?

Such situations had some historical precedents, the most recent being the high-profile attempt to boycott BP stations in the U.S. in the aftermath of that company's *Deepwater Horizon* oil spill on the Gulf Coast. Immediately, the public directed palpable anger and resentment at BP. The boycott attempt initially caused a drop-off in sales, but this turned out to be only temporary. People came to realize that the boycott mostly hurt not the BP company but the locals who owned the service station properties. Most stations are owned not by the company but by independent businesspeople. In a short time, the market, as always, decided the BP service station boycott did not work. Convenience and good service still prevailed in the minds of most motorists.

Admittedly, these boycotts involved quite different issues; one was an environmental and societal concern, and the other was a regional, avoidable, and tragic oil spill. But in any situation, efforts to convince the public via boycotts in the service station business were generally not successful. The broader question of anthropogenic (human) global warming and the morality of using gasoline in one's car would have to be addressed at a later date.

The meeting ended with the allocation of several follow-up assignments—Lavignon and I were to provide input on a statement that the corporate CEO would put out. To help with this and get a better feel for the situation, I wanted to actually visit some of the trouble spots to better form my own opinion.

This was quickly arranged.

CHAPTER V

An Activist Movement about a Lot More Than Climate

Bruce Townsend of APEXEnergy's public relations in Europe would accompany me. With his tweed jacket and ever-so-correct language, I sensed I was in the company of a very proper English gentleman who knew his business. He had come up in the organization through the marketing side, so he would have the right credentials for my interests.

Our driver was a burly representative from the security department. Given the reports we were getting from some of the demonstrations, he probably was a good choice.

We headed for one of APEX's major retail service stations. It was located in a commercial area, which also happened to be across from an open park area where some of the largest demonstrations were taking place. As we got closer to the destination, we decided to walk the rest of the way, as the streets were crowded and almost impassable for car traffic.

The crowd was a mix, mostly twenty-somethings, some carrying signs; noisier groups taunting the police; and, of course, just curious onlookers. At the APEX station, a large police presence was trying to control a very unruly crowd and not having much success. Automobile traffic was virtually at a standstill. A big, burly guy with a bullhorn, replete with a wig, suspenders, and no shirt, was egging on the crowd, first to stress that people not buy from APEX and then to reinforce the point fossil fuels were destroying the planet. The mob scene was punctuated with signs advocating the same messages but also other messages well beyond, including inequality and anticapitalism; seemingly, some people were pretty unhappy with life in general! A chaotic scene all around!

I couldn't help wondering who was coordinating all of this. Who was paying for this effort? Many sign carriers seemed almost oblivious to the purpose of the protest as they marched back and forth. Why were they there? Then there were others, seemingly more engaged, who looked like they could even be off the local university campus, not that the sightings of Gucci shoes and horn-rimmed glasses were any confirmation of that.

My curiosity about the forces behind this demonstration and other goings-on elsewhere only increased when a tall, good-looking young lady, who seemed to be one of the leaders, pushed a sign at me (saying, Capitalism Sucks! no less) and urged me to join in the protest.

Slightly annoyed, I responded, "And for what purpose? What is being accomplished?"

The tart reply was "Don't you know that fossil fuels sold by these APEX people cause emissions of CO_2, which is a greenhouse gas, and that is what is causing global warming? Our planet is burning up, and so we have to change to clean energy."

She seemed to be well informed, so I pressed on. "I presume you refer to solar and wind alternatives, but are these sources not still unreliable and considerably more expensive? Look at electric power rates in Germany as just one example."

She then shifted the narrative: "The capitalistic system is corrupt and inefficient, and in any event, the public is ignorant about this whole subject of climate change. So society will just have to be forced to accept this change and the higher costs that go with it."

The flash in her Anglo blue eyes seemed to signal some annoyance—whether it was with me or the subject, I couldn't tell. Clearly, the change agent for this societal revamp according to this crowd, was not going to be the marketplace, nor the voters, and probably not this young lady!

The crowd was becoming more raucous, and as some fireworks began exploding a few hundred yards away, we thought it was time to retreat to our car. Back in the car without incident and settled for the long drive back, I could see Bruce Townsend was pretty upset with what we had just seen.

"Just a hodgepodge mob that represented all the problems we have in our society," he blurted. "Most of this mob doesn't have the least idea of the science behind climate change. This was just an opportunity to raise hell against the system, and of course, there were some hard-core environmentalists who saw an opportunity to advance their cause."

He opined that many were not even from the London area. They had been bused in and were backed by the leftist British Labour Party and probably the United Socialist Party of the UK.

"Climate change aside, for many in this crowd, the bigger objectives are social change, equality of outcomes in the workplace, and basically an end to capitalism as we know it. This philosophy goes so far as to say our materialistic way of life has to be reversed, and instead of growth, a new term, *degrowth*, signifying a return to a simpler, less technological way of living. Shades of the hippie culture of the 1960s! In some minds, this organized attack on Big Oil, a pillar of oppressive capitalism, presented a golden opportunity."

I interrupted his tirade and posed a question. "So where does this go from here? We have a business to run, many employees, and more important, millions of customers who depend on us. Our industry is fundamental to our way of life until well into the future, so how do we deal with this climate change issue?"

Bruce pondered the questions for a moment and replied simply, "With patience, good communication, and most importantly, some basic policy changes."

"Policy changes? What do you mean by that, Bruce?"

He replied, "We would have to rethink our basic corporate position on environment and, yes, on climate change and, yes, on global warming. The fanatical left are being successful in casting our industry not only as climate change deniers but actually as obstructionists to the science of climate change. According to them, we are stuck in the past, protective of our fossil fuel industry, and opposed to new-age alternative energy sources, which, they argue, would lower greenhouse gases necessary to control global warming. Didn't our own research and engineering labs forecast this looming threat of uncontrolled CO_2 emissions as we moved into the twenty-first century? And what's worse, our critics allege we covered up this data, and now, the world is faced with the 'existential threat' to our way of life.

"Of course, there is major error and distortion of facts in all of this, but the reality is our industry and APEX, as a major player, are getting a bad rap in the court of public opinion. We need to find a way to attack these perceptions, and this means we will have to address some of our own internal corporate realities first."

Bruce had obviously done a lot of thinking on these issues. And I thought, *He is mostly right!*

Back at the office, the discussion continued. I got Lavignon involved. Clearly, many of these policy ideas and decisions to be made were well above our pay scale, but Lavignon and I knew we would have to carry these ideas and recommendations forward to senior management.

The rest of the day focused on immediate messaging to the local London media as well as preparation of communiques for the international wire services. The disruption to our business needed a strong response; otherwise, the public would give unwarranted credence to this protest movement. The protesters were in full attack mode against the very integrity of our business.

As the afternoon wore on, the public affairs team worked up various statements—on APEX's commitment to all things environmental, our history of corporate citizenship, and petroleum products' basic importance to our very way of life—to go public. Key spokespersons were identified to get this messaging out to newspapers and television. A full court press was on, but would it be enough?

Both Lavignon and I knew that while the immediate challenge was here in the UK, we had to start preparing for a much broader corporate response. Climate change had become not just a business issue but probably the seminal cultural issue of our time. We would not be able to change, nor in all probability even have an effect on this societal movement, but we would need a sound strategy to adjust to this new reality. And we would have to base this on science and the full integrity of our corporate principles.

CHAPTER VI

A Detour in the Pursuit of the Science

It was already late afternoon when one of the assistants advised me that I had a telephone call from a Ms. Forsythe, who had asked for me by name. Odd, for who could know of Scott Paladino here in London and at the APEX offices?

Curious to know, I took the call.

"My name is Eve Marie Forsythe and I was the aggressive female that confronted you earlier today"— slight giggle. "Remember, you were not too happy, and while this may seem somewhat strange, I think I have a protest perspective that you would be interested in. I will be at the Shamrock Tavern, just in front of your office building, in thirty minutes. Hope to see you, and bye-bye."

What was that? Had this happened in good old Houston, I might have thought that someone was trying to hit on me; but then, in a different country with different customs, who knew? Again, curiosity and the thought that just maybe there was something to be learned made me go.

Entering the Shamrock Tavern (in business since 1650), I recognized her immediately. No hair bun this time, her jet-black hair was down to her shoulders. Those clear blue eyes, and *gasp*, she was even better looking than I remembered.

She saw me and waved me over to her table, which I guessed was in the quieter section of the inn. It was getting pretty noisy around the bar area as the 5:00 p.m. crowd moved in. She had just a trace of a smile as she extended her hand.

"Ms. Forsythe, I presume, and what, no placards this time?"

A full smile this time, she thanked me for coming.

"So how did you find out about Scott Paladino and the APEXEnergy connection? I thought I was pretty incognito here in London."

"We have our sources." And with that, she gave me her card: *Eve Marie Forsythe—Executive Representative, Euro Public Affairs.*

"Our firm has been engaged to help organize these demonstrations. And it seems that I am pretty good at communications and public speaking—my brother says just a rabble-rouser! Be that as it may, the principals of our firm wanted me in front of these demonstrations against APEX. They pay me pretty well, so as a hired hand, I follow the script they hand me, whether I agree with the subject or not.

"So why did I contact you, and why am I telling you all this? Lord knows, because this is not my style. But there was something about you this morning—maybe your annoyance—that got me thinking. You seemed to be saying, 'Does this mindless mob—and by association, me—have any idea about what they are talking about?' You see, Mr. Paladino, as strange as it may sound coming from me, I have some serious reservations about where this movement is headed. I have spent many hours researching the subject, and frankly, I have developed some serious doubts. It seems we Brits have bought into this new religion without any questions. I sense from what I read there is a distinct counterthought, even counterargument, going on in the States. You seem to be saying there is no settled science, and considerable skepticism, on the whole subject.

"Indeed, Mr. Paladino, I have to apologize for this impertinent intrusion on your time, but I thought it was worth the risk to get your views on the subject. Go ahead, and I will understand if your first question is, 'Does your mother know you are here?' or more to the point, 'You are probably in the wrong business!'" Then she gave a full-throated laugh.

Ave Maria! There I was with this intelligent, articulate, very beautiful young lady, and she wanted to talk about climate change.

I quickly replied, "Of course. Doesn't everyone want to talk about climate change? But it would be easier to discuss over dinner, if your schedule permits."

She said yes.

Even though it was Friday night, we were able to get seated at a nearby French restaurant because of a last-minute cancellation. With a glass of Beaujolais in hand, we continued our conversation.

She was somewhat surprised to learn that my thinking on the climate change subject was still evolving. I was troubled by the science, or lack thereof, behind global warming. Yes, a gradual warming had been taking place since the late nineteenth century, but all the empirical data said that this trend upward had stalled out in about 1998. The first two decades in our twenty-first century had shown essentially little or no further increase. Still, various environmental groups and even the prestigious IPCC of the UN were in denial on this and holding to the narrative of further temperature increases of 2–4°C (4–7°F) by the end of this century. These projections were based on the numerous supercomputer models, and these sources had been pretty inaccurate in recent history. There were, therefore, some questions about the science for this theory. Then, we were constantly being reminded that CO_2, a greenhouse gas (GHG), is constantly building in the atmosphere, and therefore, temperatures have to increase. I was not sure about that conclusion. *Does temperature follow CO_2 buildup, or is it the reverse?* And at that, while CO_2 is a GHG, at less than half of 1 percent (0.046) of all gases in the atmosphere, it is a minor amount.

"Does this very minor concentration have the ability to affect our planet's temperature, and by such a large amount? And if CO_2 has such control, where is the empirical data to support this claim? We in the oil business are trying to assess these issues and the implications for our industry, so you can see our thinking is evolving."

Suddenly, I realized I had gotten carried away, totally engrossed in my world. How boring this must have sounded to this young lady, but the expression on her face said the opposite. She seemed genuinely interested as she intervened. "But what of all the prominent people, scientists at your prestigious universities, many of them professing support for these activist claims?"

I replied, "I am so glad you said *many*, but be assured that there are many others who remain skeptical. Keep in mind this whole enviro movement has become a huge business attracting many billions of dollars from investors, especially governments. Worldwide, it is estimated that this movement employs tens of thousands of people directly or indirectly. Universities dare not espouse denial or even skepticism of this so-called science if they want to attract or even maintain funding for the earth science and environmental departments. Reducing carbon from the atmosphere has a feel-good quality and believability, and then you see the likes of Leonardo DiCaprio, Al Gore, and Barack Obama piling on, and you start to wonder. It seems the vast majority of support for this new activism always comes from the ideological left. So maybe this is more a political movement?"

She continued, "But we hear all the time—seems like at least once a week—how when there is another major storm event, the various organizations and their scientists are always blaming global warming. Is this so?"

"I don't think these reports are supported by the actual data. In North America, weather data records over the most recent period—the last seventy years, in fact—indicate an amazing consistency in the average number and intensity of major weather events. I say *average* because you can have small deviations year to year, but mean averages per decade don't show much deviation. What is happening, and gets everybody's attention, is the increasing economic destruction of these events. There are much larger populations living ever closer to forests and waterways and the oceans, so the cost impacts are multiplied.

"The skeptics, or rather 'nonbelievers,' would argue that climate change, triggered by solar variability, is always at work and is what really causes these weather events. Since the phenomenon of climate change has been going on for billions of years, I don't think it is about to change."

Our discussions continued well into a second bottle of Beaujolais. It was rather fascinating how one so beautiful could be so interested in such a dry subject. But then, in a way, she was in the business too.

Regardless, I knew I had to see her again, but how? She must have a boyfriend. Bright, good lookers like her always have boyfriends, so they must always be busy. Gathering my courage after another sip of wine, I blurted out, "Forsythe, would you be able to meet me tomorrow afternoon for some London sightseeing?"

To my relief, she said, "Palodin, it would be a pleasure!" Then, in her delightful English accent, she added, "I will pick you up at your hotel at 2:00 p.m."

At my hotel? Was there anything about me she did not know?

And where did this *Palodin* come from? Nobody had ever called me that. But then, I had never met anybody quite like her.

CHAPTER VII

Life Gets More Complicated and Interesting

Saturday morning, 8:00 o'clock, it was all hands on deck at our APEXEnergy London offices. We got hit pretty hard in the Friday night news cycle, particularly by the liberal-left news media. We had to respond, and maybe more important, we had to try to get out ahead with our own messaging. Just responding to the activists would never work. And we had a window of opportunity: Sunday TV shows were anxious to hear from us. And fortunately, we had some pretty talented people across our public relations, finance, and planning departments, where several had extensive experience in TV and media presentations. Most of those presentations tended to be on the energy outlook and the importance of fossil fuels right up to the year 2040.

The focus had to be, and would be, a lot more than just dry statistics, but those would be a good starting point because we had to emphasize the importance of petroleum energy. And most important, our own company data had to be backed up by data from the International Energy Agency (IEA)

We spent most of the morning on how to best focus the message—not exactly exciting stuff for most viewers, but I could see that these guys had been down this road before and were pretty good at making a case.

Energy demand in the UK and globally would illustrate how our economic system heavily relied on fossil fuels and how the much-maligned CO_2 levels had actually fallen in Europe and the U.S. since 2005. Interestingly, the latter phenomenon had little to do with government policies and everything to do with new technologies from the private sector, such as cleaner-burning, natural gas–displacing coal in power plants, and more efficient engines in the transportation sector.

After starting with the data background, we would lead into some specific programs APEXEnergy was working on in support of the environment, including CO_2-mitigation efforts in our company operations—carbon capture and sequestration, biofuel use, et cetera. We had some short video clips describing these programs, which we would blend into the presentations. It would be important to emphasize these areas as solid testimony to our long record of good corporate citizenship, both locally and internationally.

The anti-oil crowd was making some pretty absurd claims, and we would answer with some actual empirical data, something that was amazingly absent in the heat of this controversy.

And then it was 2:00 p.m. In front of the hotel, there was Eve Marie with a broad smile and a *cheerio* … that penetrating gaze. She was even more stunning than my recall from the night before, or maybe just my imagination.

"And so, Mr. Paladino, where would you like to visit?"

"You lead the way, beautiful. Remember, I am just an ignorant visitor."

She then recommended a visit to the British Museum, which was not too far from where we were. "That is, if you won't mind all the American tourists."

I suggested that I could probably handle it.

I had heard so much about this museum, sometimes described as the *museum of the world*. With over two million years of history, artifacts, and cultures, clearly a month would not be enough to see it all.

As we traversed the many galleries of the Parthenon sculptures, Egyptian mummies, and even dinosaurs, I could not help thinking of the role that an ever-changing climate must have played in the rise and fall of these ancient civilizations.

As if on cue, was there not a table set up at a gallery entrance, identified as the British Historical Society distributing pamphlets titled "Mother Nature, Ancient World to the Present"? Opening the brochure, I saw there in the centerfold a chart Fig. 1, no less, depicting temperature data, warming and cooling across the centuries. Even more fascinating was the correlation of warm periods with the heights of the world's greatest civilizations! Intriguing!

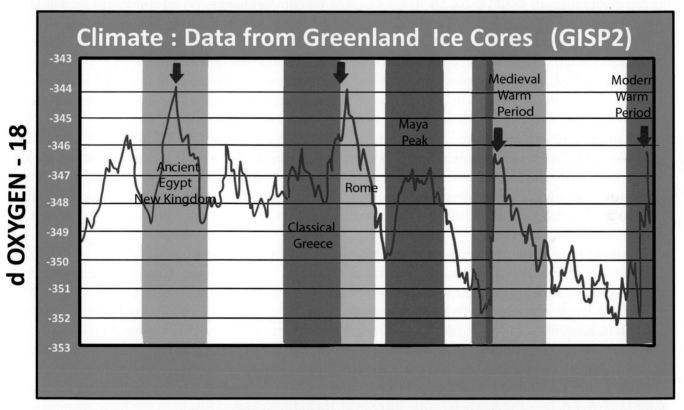

Fig. 1. Climatic variations and effect on civilizations

"But, Scott, where do they get this data, and how do we know that this is all true? After all, this goes back many centuries," said Eve Marie.

"Well, as noted, these Greenland ice cores have proven to be very accurate, and carbon dating, solar activity data, and technologies used for these sources have gotten better in recent years. The science is now supported with actual empirical data. And look at this chart more carefully. You will notice the red arrows on the temperature peaks on the graph, always followed by major cooling periods. But, beautiful lady, look what this article goes on to say: 'Over the last 6,000 years, like clockwork, these peaks occurred every 1,030 years, with the latest being the year 2007.' According to this analysis, unless different this time, our temperature trend now will be going downward, not up as the climate alarmists are saying.

"And the article even cites a Russian astrophysicist, head of the International Space Station, who publicly predicted that a mini ice age is on the way now! Wow. I have not seen this analysis before—brings into question the whole idea of CO_2 emissions' effect on temperature."

Three hours had passed quickly, and Eve Marie broke into my thought train to advise that we were getting beyond afternoon tea—couldn't let that happen. And with that, we left the museum, and she led me up a side street to what she called a proper English tearoom. As we settled down to tea and little cucumber sandwiches (really?), the conversation continued.

"You know, Palodin, I remember from my long-ago ancient civilization studies at university that the rise of great civilizations was marked with warm temperatures when agriculture flourished, and then there were the cold periods that followed when even food became scarce and people were unhappy. This is often referred to as the Dark Ages, like in the 1600s. I hope that we are not going back to some cold period, or worse. The world population has grown tenfold since those miserable medieval times. Yet, humans are very adaptable, and we do have modern-day technology. Even so, one would think the impact on agriculture and food supply for ten billion people could be disastrous!"

Then she broke out that disarming smile and said, "Listen, Palodin, I never thought that taking you to our great museum would end with another treatise on climate change. When you Yanks get a hold of something, you just don't let go … Just kidding. This has been very interesting. I'm impressed."

With that, she reached over and took my hand and said, "And you know what else London is famous for? Great Indian restaurants. If you would like, we can go to one not far from here."

As we walked down the narrow streets toward the restaurant, we fell into total silence. I was thinking about how very pleasant it was to be with this person and just how comfortable she made me feel. And with that, I had just a fleeting thought about where this short relationship was going.

I had had one serious relationship when in college, and my mind flashed back to Marina, a beautiful girl. We had talked about getting married as soon as I graduated. By then, it seemed to me we should wait a little until I was in a job and earning some money. This didn't work for her, and lo and behold, six weeks later, she was engaged to be married to a local TV personality. So much for that "undying love" idea!

But this English girl was so different: intellectual, very sharp, humorous, and physically very attractive. But really, who was she?

It wasn't long before we were seated at the Barbary, one of the better-known Indian restaurants in London. We ordered, and my curiosity could wait no longer. "Miss Forsythe, please excuse my candor, but who is Eve Marie, this beautiful English girl that I have met here in London?"

After a laugh, she replied, "Well, I am not a third party"—another deep-throated laugh—"just an English lass, twenty-eight years old, a fine-arts graduate from Cambridge University. And yatty, yatty, you don't want to hear more boring details. I do know you Yanks are big on sports, so I will admit to playing a fair game of tennis, and did get to the semifinals one year in the university games.

"On a more serious note, I have been lucky to have a great family. My father is a lawyer—we call them *barristers* over here—and has been quite successful, including a high position in the Blair government. Mother is a psychologist and has her own clinic. Brother James is a carefree soul and recent engineering graduate who, as far as I can tell, is doing a major in London nightlife. That should change pretty soon as he joins the corporate world and gets hit with the realities of the real world.

"And as for me and the not-so-boring details? I guess you might be wondering about my boyfriends and maybe even why I am not married at the ripe old age of twenty-eight. Well, until recently, I was *involved*, as they like to say, with a rather handsome, charming Frenchman who is a pretty famous soccer—football—star. Until recently, he played for Fulham FC, a UK Premier League team here in London, which has not performed well in recent years. In retrospect, I guess he was a little too romantic because he seemed to be back and forth to Paris quite often just to visit his mother. My suspicions were confirmed when a photo of him with an 'acquaintance' appeared in *Paris Match* magazine, and she certainly was not his mother! That was it, and then he was recently sold to an Italian League team. Good riddance!

"So you see, I was jilted!" She laughed. "And oh, by the way, that Fulham team is owned by an American, Shah Khan. And maybe you already know, he is also the owner of one of your professional American football teams, called the Jacksonville Jaguars. The Jaguars have a big fan club here in London, and hallelujah, would you believe, I did go to see them play last year at Wembley Stadium. I must say very exciting but a little complicated with all the rules.

"We Brits seem to have a certain affinity for things American. Maybe it has always been that way, but even more so since World War II. In the case of our family, there is a bigger reason. My paternal grandfather came over to England in the waning days of that war as a young B-52 bomber pilot. By war's end, he had already met Marie, who became my grandmother, and decided to settle down in England. He had a long and successful executive career with the Rolls-Royce company. But more important, he became a very special presence in our family, attractive, humorous, and wise. Everybody admired him.

"So, Palodin, here we are … you think you are with just an English girl, but you see, I am part American!" Another very infectious laugh.

I responded, "How could I not have suspected, with such a fine accent!"

She continued, "Changing the subject, there is something else. I have been reassigned to lead a project we have been working on: a motivational speaking course with a major car company client. Our organization has just decided to back away from the global warming crowd because of critical feedback from several clients. In any event, we pretty much accomplished what that contract called for."

"When we first met, Eve Marie, you indicated some skepticism about the goals of the climate activists that you were working for. Maybe you now feel more freedom to talk to that? I take it you do believe in environmentalism?"

"Of course I believe in the enviro fundamentals. Doesn't everybody? We are all stewards of this planet, and I believe we have individual and collective responsibility for taking whatever steps necessary to ensure clean air, clean water, sanitation, and antilittering, and even opting for best standards on all things visual. Where I struggle is with this activist movement, which essentially has been hijacked for more extreme purposes. How so? you might ask. What extremes? To answer this, you have to identify the actors and what they seek to achieve. To be sure, there are some sincere believers, idealists that think they are doing God's work in an effort to save humankind and the planet as we know it. But there are many more nefarious elements who see this as an opportunity to make fundamental changes to our society.

"These groups oppose the very basis of our prosperity, starting with capitalism itself but including many fundamental belief systems such as religion, family, and even our basic educational system. This is more than a new green religion. It is a call for basic societal change, neo-Marxism. I have seen these people up close. They are radical extremists whose target is destruction of the existing status quo, and there are many examples, such as chaotic riots in our cities, defunding the police, and critical race theories in education. And the greatest symbol of that status quo is the business corporation, the very foundation of capitalism, which brings us back to your APEXEnergy. You are today's target, and I am sure there will be another one tomorrow. Carbon emissions and existential threat may resonate with the public, but this movement is about much more than that! And Mr. Paladino, that is my little rant for today, but you know you are partly to blame, with your many insights on anthropogenic effects on climate. I'm just being a good student!"

Rant or no, her fervor transfixed me. When she got fired up, those eyes were absolutely flashing!

The evening wore on with more cocktails and a lot of conversation, but then it was getting late. I didn't want it to end, but it had to.

As we waited for our taxi, she informed me that she had obtained two tickets for the London Symphony Orchestra's Sunday afternoon concert tomorrow. They would perform Tchaikovsky's *Pathetique Symphony* at the Barbican concert hall. And just when I was wondering how, or if, I would see her again.

After a short taxi ride, I walked her to the door of her apartment, and as I moved to kiss her cheek, she turned, and her lips were fully on mine. We embraced and held the kiss for long, incredible seconds.

I was going to marry this girl!

I hurried back to the waiting taxi.

CHAPTER VIII

From ESG to CA 100+ and Then …. Tchaikovsky?

Back in my hotel room, the phone light was on, indicating a message. Jim Lavignon had called and wanted me to meet him for a breakfast meeting at 8:00 the next morning.

When I arrived at the hotel coffee shop, Jim was already seated off in one corner. He wasted no time.

"Scott, the exec committee at Houston headquarters has been in contact with me, and they want a priority update on where we are on ESG [environmental, social, and governance] and also this latest indexing, Climate Action 100+."

It seemed that an activist shareholder group was pushing for more information on APEX's position on these ratings and suggesting our silence was indicative of passive climate change policies. The particular investor group included several large state pension funds who, combined, held over 20 percent of APEX's outstanding stock. They were even pushing for two seats on our board, and with our annual meeting coming up in six weeks, this had become a serious concern.

"The Excom wants our assessment and recommendations on all this by next week. And Scott, I know you were working on this issue over recent months, so give me your thoughts on where we stand."

"Right, Jim. In fact, I was getting deep into the weeds on all this when this London trip came up rather suddenly. As you know, an ESG metric for a company is a so-called measure of that company's sustainability (in APEX's case, adaptability to changing energy trends) and the ethics of investment in that company. Pretty general term, but increasingly being used by investors as an indicator of corporate behavior and even future financial performance. ESG is thought to be growing as more of the millennial generation makes up the pool of investors. But in my digging into the subject, it by no means has general acceptance as a sound metric. Some individual investors and even major fund investors reject ESG for several reasons. First and foremost, the assessment is highly subjective, with indexes published from several sources using differing criteria and weighting and therefore having little agreement on assigned rating values, even on the same company.

"Also, most blue chip companies like APEX already have a major focus on our responsibilities toward our corporate stakeholders, be they customers, communities, employees, or shareholders. And since our major responsibility is maximizing profits for these stakeholders, we cannot accomplish this if we ignore main factors key to that success, such as employee concerns, legal, and community outreach, among the many issues that make up good corporate citizenship.

"It's worth noting that Japan's Government Pension Investment Fund, the world's largest with around $1.6 trillion under management, is abandoning trendy ESG investment. 'The strategy was a financial loser'—a direct quote from fund managers. They went on to say, 'We can't sacrifice returns for the sake of buying environmental names or ESG names.' So nothing clear cut here, though it does get attention in U.S. financial markets and increasingly is being used as an investor criterion.

"I think the main driver behind this initiative is the environmental [in ESG] and getting more corporate buy-in for a proactive push on climate change. And this is even more the case on the latest climate index du jour you mentioned, Climate Action 100+. This is probably an even more insidious attack. It's described as an 'investor initiative to ensure the world's largest greenhouse gas emitters (includes countries) take necessary action on climate change.' This is an activist movement that is really just an outgrowth of the 2015 Paris Climate Accord (which accomplished nothing except talk) and is belatedly targeting countries and companies, who they say are lagging in efforts to curb emissions, as they build pressure for the next global climate conference planned for Glasgow, Scotland, in October 2021.

"Unfortunately, Jim, as we all know, this is the world of climate change and its growing presence, and influence, in our corporate world. Of course, the world economy runs on energy, and over 80 percent of that energy now comes from low-cost fossil fuels, which one way or another have to be backed out to make room for significantly higher-cost, less efficient renewables such as solar and wind. The not-so-subtle objective of these rating schemes is to dry up capital investment sources for our fossil fuel–based industry, or at least to drive up the cost of this capital. This, in turn, translates to lower fossil fuel supply, higher prices, and less competition for alternate energy sources."

Lavignon then questioned what metrics were being used and who was setting them. Various organizations, some well known, such as Dow Jones, were involved on ESG. CA 100+ used Tracker to rate entities on their emissions. We were already in touch with these providers and how they rated APEX and were waiting on some information. I would be following up on this as soon as we got back to Houston and let him know immediately.

Our discussions had run on for several hours, and now, I was running late for a very important date. Fortunately, Lavignon had to leave, so I sent a message to Eve Marie for us to meet at the Barbican Centre.

And there she was, dressed in a black suit with a white scarf casually draped around her head. Spectacular! Her pantsuit was just tight enough not to hide important details of what was obviously a very athletic body. With my arm around her waist, I kissed her first on one cheek, then the other, eliciting her usual deep-throated laugh.

"And so, Mr. Paladino, do you like the music of Pyotr Ilyich Tchaikovsky?"

"Of course," I replied.

My music trajectory was pretty limited. But Tchaikovsky's sixth symphony, the famous *Pathetique*, happened to be a favorite, mainly because of my mother. She loved classical music, and growing up, we always had a modest collection of CDs playing in the house. She was also a pretty accomplished pianist and at one point had thought that was where my potential talent lay. So a very patient piano teacher encouraged me along until my darker angels prevailed and I took up ice hockey, where, I might add, I was a little more successful. But in retrospect, it did seem that a serious attraction to mostly classical music had taken hold and that interest had only increased over the years.

I had never seen a live Symphony orchestra, much less the famous London Symphony Orchestra, play the sixth. This would be special, made only more so by the beautiful girl at my side. And it was, as was the rest of the day destined to be.

By late afternoon, we were headed to the Savoy hotel for drinks at the bar and then dinner. It was not too crowded, and I was able to get the barman to switch channels so we could see the APEX interviews over recent protests.

Jon Lester, a senior VP, articulated our position very well and then, as we Americans like to say, hit a home run when challenged on the "failures" of capitalism. His retort: "Compared to what—the collapse of Soviet communism, Venezuelan or Western European social democracies, or maybe Cuban communism? Capitalism, like democracy, can seem, and at times is, a little messy. But it espouses opportunity and reward like no other system and can be largely credited with raising hundreds of millions of people worldwide out of poverty over the last century."

Eve Marie was impressed as she remarked, "Big corporations train their people well!"

Our back-and-forth banter suddenly became serious as I explained that my work in London had just about finished and I would be heading back to the States this coming Wednesday. This might be our last meeting for a while; her hand moved to cover mine as we fell into what seemed like a rather heavy silence.

We could not leave it this way. My inquiry to the maître d' uncovered that right next door to the hotel was a very popular nightclub, Lucero and the Mariachis—lots of Latin music, but this being London, also some traditional Western music.

The mariachi concert lived up to its billing. You can't listen to Mexican music and not be happy. The rendition of el famoso "El Caballo Blanco" was special, made more so by a patron who invited himself to the microphone to sing the lyrics in perfect Spanish. Eve Marie and I both concluded he must be a plant. But it was funny, and after the requisite drink of tequila, it all got more humorous.

And then the dance music began, a slower rhythm, which seemed to suit both of us. Holding her close was everything I imagined, and pretty soon, it seemed only she and I were on the dance floor. Lost in thought, lost in time, we held each other ever closer. We knew this could not end.

Then wordlessly, we walked back to my hotel, and we would spend the night together, embracing like there was no tomorrow. But of course there always is, and when I awakened early, she was gone.

No, not possible, I thought. *Must have been a dream!* But then a note on the mirror:

Duty calls, early morning meeting, talk later. Love you! —E. M.

The last days before Lavignon's and my British Air departure were hectic as we raced to finish several reports. My nonstop thinking about Eve Marie did not make those days any easier. In the midst of all the turmoil and acrimony here in London, she had been a great reprieve, a sounding board for my thoughts and even theories on the subject of climate. Her intellectual curiosity had reached into aspects I hadn't ever thought about. And beyond all of that, a deep emotional bond had taken hold.

But now, I had to get my head together, get focused. The agenda ahead was going to be difficult enough.

British Airways flight 630, London Heathrow to Houston, USA, was finally called, and of course, long lines were everywhere. But then, "Scott, Scott," said a familiar voice from way back in the crowd. That could only be one person.

Turning quickly, I saw Eve waving frantically. I raced back through the long queue and in one motion gathered her in my arms and embraced her with a long, lingering kiss. "I love you, Eve. This is not the end, just the beginning. I will call you from Houston. Make sure you answer the phone, lass!"

"Oh, yes. And I, too, love you, Scott," she replied.

And then I had to go. I was the last one on the plane before the cabin door was closed.

"Hey, Scott, what was that all about?" asked Jim Lavignon.

"Just a protester that I ran into at the London demonstrations," I replied with a smile.

CHAPTER IX

✳

When Climate Change Becomes Religion

The ten-hour flight from London to Houston would be made more pleasant by our first-class accommodations. Company policy permitted this upgrade on any flights longer than five hours. And when the cabin steward greeted us with a glass of champagne, it indeed seemed first class.

It didn't take long to get back to the discussion of events of recent days. Lavignon expressed concern, as he put it, with not only the protest movement against our company but also our seeming lack of preparedness or strategy to provide some explanation, or even pushback, to the public. He pointed a finger at not just APEXEnergy UK but ourselves in Houston HQ. We would need to reach a better description of the climate change issue as it affected our industry and develop a strategy to address the problem. And this had to happen quickly.

He then advised that a report on our London visit, with some preliminary recommendations, was to be made to the management committee next Wednesday at 10:00 p.m. He wanted me to assist him with this presentation. In fact, it had been decided that I would make the PowerPoint presentation. I decided that the one glass of champagne was enough, as my mind had already started to race ahead to the preparation that would be required.

A growing segment of the American public was starting to believe that climate warming was real and was caused by humans' use of fossil fuels and resulting CO_2 emissions, which would lead to an overheating of planet Earth and, ominously, the virtual extinction of the human race by the end of the century. The climate activists promoting this narrative further argued that the only remedy was an aggressive mitigation effort by society at all levels, directed by the government at business and the ordinary citizen. According to this new doctrine, it was imperative to reduce the carbon footprint to near net zero in all countries and thereby hold the maximum temperature rise through the rest of this century to less than 1°C.

The fact that this theory had questionable scientific support was irrelevant. Much had already been invested in this industry, and the movement must proceed. It had become very political and even ideological, so it even transcended rational dialogue. The movement had achieved true religious status.

One wondered when the public would start paying serious attention to the issues involved: when electric power rates doubled, when electric grids failed because of unreliable alternative energy sources, when higher taxes were imposed to fund government subsidies on EVs and inefficient grid systems, when transportation costs went up, or maybe when an ever-larger, intrusive government sought to implement the Green New Deal?

Much of this narrative was being pushed by special-interest groups ranging from politicians to universities and private-sector businesses, all with clearly identifiable agendas. This was not to say there were no sincere and honest believers who truly thought that they were doing God's work!

But back to the present: *What should our message be to the Excom next week?*

CHAPTER X

The Corporate Process at Work

Lowell Anderson, CEO and president of APEXEnergy, had called the meeting with most of the executive committee, including vice presidents for production, refining, and marketing, to be in attendance.

Mr. Anderson was a tall, slim Texan, well tanned, which fit the description that he was a golfer and a pretty good one at that, reportedly with a single-digit handicap. He looked to be in his early fifties and had graduated from the Colorado School of Mines with a degree in geology. In his career at APEXEnergy, he had worked through the ranks of exploration and production, which was a pretty usual path for senior executives at major oil companies. The big money in the oil business has always been in the business's upstream end. Discovering and developing good crude oil reserves usually means success.

The meeting was called to order, and the head of planning and logistics began with a short overview of business performance by geographical area. This was followed by Jim Lavignon, who made some introductory remarks on the climate change issue as a lead-in to my presentation.

In addition to the world headlines against APEXEnergy in the UK, secondary demonstrations against our operations in Europe, in California, and in Toronto, Canada, were occurring. While these MeToo protests were not as chaotic as in London, they were generating bad press everywhere, readily fed by a sympathetic media.

And then came my turn. To say that I was nervous would be the understatement of the year. All these senior executives appeared sympathetic to the nervous young man about to speak and maybe just a little curious about how he was going to handle the challenge.

As silly as it may seem, I calmed myself with a simple thought: maybe I was the most junior person in the room, but probably, I knew more about the issues and the dynamics of environmentalism than anybody else in the room. A little arrogant perhaps, but it seemed to settle my nerves for the moment, and I began the well-rehearsed presentation.

I led off with a careful recounting of the events in London, my field trip, and our best assessment of the prime actors and agendas driving this movement. This was followed by some discussion and questioning on what the UK team was doing to confront the problems. I gave an overview of our work with UK management, including getting the message out to the media and other important groups and making some progress. By the end of the previous week, the UK *Telegraph* and even the UK *Times* had seemed to be coming down hard on the mayhem. Most interesting from our point of view were the positive comments on our company, our long record of good corporate citizenship, and above all, the importance of the hydrocarbon industry now and into the foreseeable future.

With some trepidation, I approached the last point in my presentation: APEXEnergy needed more specifics and clarity on its climate change position. "As a major oil company, do we believe in man-made global warming? Are CO_2 emissions from fossil fuels that we sell causing a warming trend? If so, to what extent do we agree with end-of-century cataclysmic temperature forecasts?

"Do we have a mitigation program both in the company and for external public consumption of petroleum? Some of our industry competitors are already announcing plans to phase out petroleum in favor of alternative forms of energy. Most in the private business sector have signed on to the green environmental programs with almost daily statements to achieve net-zero carbon levels.

"Given all this, what should our public policy be, and how should that be communicated? In our opinion, these are the major concerns for APEXEnergy going forward, and they must be addressed. Gentlemen, that ends my presentation."

The silence was finally broken when Anderson said, "Mr. Paladino, is there any direct correlation between CO_2 levels in the atmosphere and the earth's temperature?"

This was getting right at the science, and I was ready. I replied, "Sir, there is some skepticism on this question even in the scientific community, but I will say there are studies from very reputable sources that conclude there is no correlation between CO_2 levels and temperature."

"Then, Mr. Paladino, what is the purpose of mitigation at great cost to the company, and society at large, if there is no connection between CO_2 levels and temperature?"

"Sir, I cannot answer that right now. We are in the midst of great controversy on exactly that issue. We are working on basic underlying science here and getting more information on this subject in order to make the right recommendations for APEXEnergy."

Anderson then adjourned the meeting but not before saying that the Marketing and Public Affairs departments would head a task force on Mission Environment with Messrs. Lavignon and Paladino as key members of the study group.

The executive committee would reconvene in two weeks to hear a definitive analysis and recommendations. The urgency of this mandate was not lost on anyone.

The following days involved many discussions and short meetings, and none more important than those with J. Peter Potter, Anderson's executive assistant. He had received some pretty specific directions on what was expected from our team.

Management was concerned that climate change had become the central issue of our times, as it concerned the oil industry, our company, and indeed our whole society. We as an industry had not paid enough attention to the issue, in good part because we had felt that the science was not there as to both causes and solutions. We had become passive observers, and now, the issue had gotten ahead of us.

So where was the science on climate change and global warming, and what empirical data supported these issues? The team was assembled, and each of the areas was delegated. The focal point had to be unpacking the science, and given my environmental and engineering background, I was designated to lead this effort.

As we plunged into the subject, I was amazed to find the extensive work, including scientific papers already in the public domain, on every dimension of global warming and climate change, much of it directly challenging what the new green religion was saying. The range of these studies covered the whole climate spectrum, from rising sea levels to coral reefs, melting glaciers, and the frequency and severity of major weather events. Most phenomena clearly pointed to natural climate change variability as unsurprisingly driving climate and weather.

The literature and many online presentations were replete with opposing views on the whole subject of climate change. People at the highest levels of academia seemed in disagreement, but interestingly, semantics and connections with vested interests were clearly in play. So where were this much-advertised "settled science" and the "97 percent of all scientists' consensus" coming from?

With a little investigation—and I didn't have to look too far—I found that many in this activist movement had little data, or even a rational basis, for the why of global warming, so they would frequently escape to the convenient refuge that "nearly all scientists say it is so; therefore, it must be so."

This claim had been refuted by none other than the Global Warming Petition Project at the Oregon Institute of Science and Medicine, which had obtained signatures on a declaration from 31,478 American scientists, 9,021 of whom had PhDs. The declaration stated, "There is no convincing scientific evidence that human releases of carbon dioxide, methane or other greenhouse gases are causing or will in the foreseeable future cause catastrophic heating of the earth's atmosphere and disruption of the climate." It is rather doubtful that these signees, from one source, compose the 3 percent of nonbelievers.

And as to the 2,500 "leading scientists" referenced as supporting the 2004 IPCC report? In fact, this listing included many politicians, nonscientists, and even scientists who objected to details of the final report and who demanded that their names be removed, but they were refused.

Hardly ringing endorsements by recognized experts in the scientific community.

CHAPTER XI

Bridge to Reality on Climate Science

The debate surrounding anthropogenic global warming has been with us for decades as far back as the 1970s, but really became mainstream in our national consciousness in the late 1990s. Opinions would vary, but perhaps Al Gore's arrival on the scene with his signature documentary *An Inconvenient Truth* in the early 2000s was what really ignited the controversy. Even before that fiction, British prime minister Margaret Thatcher improbably and accidentally played an even more important role. Her battle with the striking coal miners and the Organization of the Petroleum Exporting Countries (OPEC) led her to convince the British people that clean nuclear power was the way to go in lessening dependence on fossil fuels. This made her a natural anti-CO_2 ally and gave this developing climate religion early credibility.

The nexus of the argument by this new religion's adherents was that the slow warming trend since the preindustrial late nineteenth century had accelerated with ever-increasing CO_2 emissions. And based on computer model projections, temperatures would reach untenable levels by 2050, and the situation would be catastrophic by the end of this century. Carbon emissions from the use of fossil fuels were the culprit, and we would face an existential threat to our very existence if we didn't take immediate steps to reduce these emissions. It would be an Armageddon scenario!

Our task force would lay out the empirical evidence for or against this thesis while simultaneously examining changing energy market trends and best strategy for Apex going forward. We would accomplish this by addressing :

- The facts of climate change
- Energy demand outlook by sector
- The increasing role of renewables
- Strategy recommendations for APEXEnergy
- Communication to the public

CHAPTER XII

······················ ✺ ······················

Unpacking the Science of Climate Change

Understanding present climate change requires some understanding of past climatic change; unequivocally, the earth's climate has always been changing. Changes in climate have been going on for billions of years on planet Earth. These changes occur in cycles, alternately warming and cooling as illustrated in the chart Fig. 2. While these cycles have been going on for millions of years, the chart only shows a relatively recent 100,000 years. The latest climate-mania temperature spike is rather trivial, at least compared to ancient Egyptian warm periods. Interesting, too, the long-term trend is heading downward!

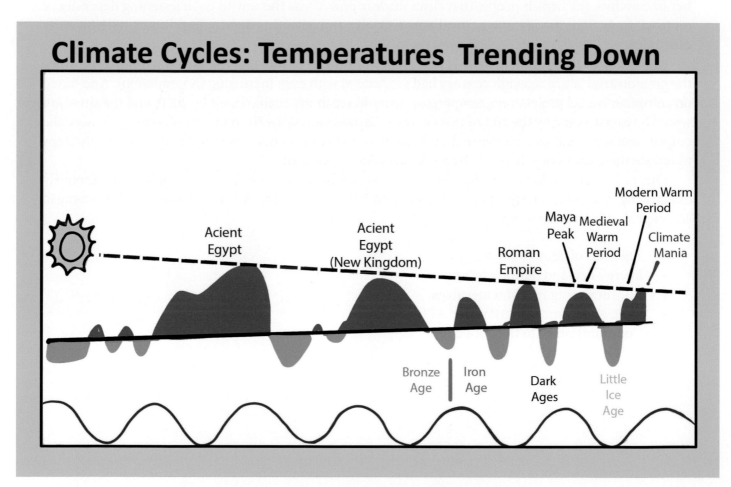

Fig. 2. Temperature trends across the centuries

But what of changed conditions, such as the large increases in fossil fuel use? Does not this increase in CO_2 levels portend further increases in temperature? All the supercomputer model projections say yes. Yet to even the casual observer, the opposite seems to be happening. While emissions have been growing exponentially all throughout the twentieth century (5 bT/yr to 35 bT/yr), temperature growth has been only modest and actually ceased to increase in the twenty-first century's first two decades. During the 1970s, temperatures actually decreased, and it was widely reported that we may be entering a new ice age.

Here, we had these large cyclical changes in temperature over many thousands of years. Was CO_2 or something else driving these changes?

This was Anderson's question too, so this had to be a good place to start.

CHAPTER XIII

CO$_2$ Emissions and Global Warming

Carbon dioxide (CO$_2$) is an odorless, colorless gas and is one of the most important gases on earth. All plants and trees depend on CO$_2$, plus sunlight and water, in order to grow and flourish, providing humans with the food we eat and, most important, the oxygen we breathe. All life owes its very existence to the presence of carbon dioxide in our atmosphere.

At that, CO$_2$ is a minor gas in the atmosphere, with less than half of 1 percent (0.04) of all gases. Nitrogen (78 percent) and oxygen (21 percent) predominate, as per the chart Fig. 3. Some of the sunlight reaching the earth's surface gets reflected back to the atmosphere as infrared rays, in turn gets absorbed by this CO$_2$ layer, and allegedly then reflects back to cause warming.

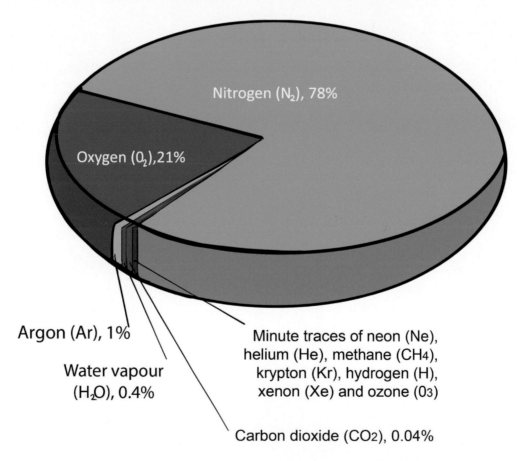

Fig. 3. Carbon dioxide (CO2) is a minor gas in the Earth's atmosphere

Even though, as mentioned, CO$_2$ is a greenhouse gas and recently has become rather notorious, allegedly the heat-trapping gas primarily responsible for global warming. Furthermore, these carbon emissions have grown significantly since the early part of the last century and are mostly due to anthropogenic (human) activity. As can be seen from the following chart Fig. 4, this growth trend is expected to continue into the 2040 time frame, in tandem with continuing high demand for fossil fuels.

Mitigation efforts already underway, and the growing role of renewable energy is reflected in these forecasts.

ENERGY RELATED CO₂ EMISSIONS BY REGION

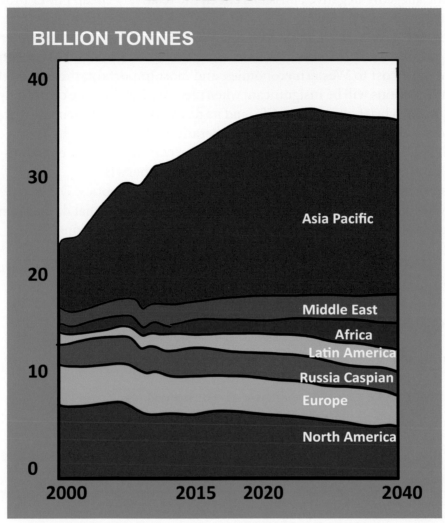

Fig. 4. World emissions continue to grow even as Europe/North America diminish

As can be observed from the chart, the developed economies of the West will continue to lower their outputs while the still-developing economies of the Asia Pacific region, mostly China and India, will more than offset any gains in the West. Although the U.S. is the world's largest economy, China has much higher emissions, nearly double the U.S.'s emissions.

U.S. emissions have dropped by 18 percent since 2005, mainly due to advances in technology and coal conversion to natural gas in power plants, reducing emissions to just a fraction of China and India's combined output.

China says all the right things about reducing carbon emissions and is even lauded for its solar technology leadership, as well as initiatives in other energies, while at the same time, it continues its aggressive program of new coal-fired power plants. Existential threats or no, China's first priority is electrification to bring its remaining millions out of poverty, which is understandable. Nevertheless, the following report is interesting and invites a broader perspective.

- China has two-thousand-plus coal-fired power plants.
- China is building (or planning) one thousand more (50 percent increase).
- The USA has fifteen (major conversion to clean-burning natural gas).
- The USA is building zero more.

Aside from the allegedly negative emissions effect, the relatively cheap power provides China with significant advantages in world trade.

To emphasize, the developed economies in the West (comprising essentially North America and Europe) have already reduced carbon emissions to a fraction of the combined Asian output. Further cuts will only come at great cost to Western economies, and most important, the potential for meaningful further emission reductions will be insignificant when measured against the continuing growth in Asia.

The forgoing is but a brief overview of CO_2 and its role in the ongoing narrative of global warming. According to the activists, the slow increase in temperatures (1.7°F) since the 1860s, coupled with the explosive growth in CO_2 emissions, could lead to only one conclusion: CO_2 emissions must be causing global warming! How could any reasonable person conclude otherwise?

But wait … science should always be questioned, always have skeptics. Otherwise, it is not science. And there has always been a considerable body of thought and scientists that do question this conclusion. The skepticism derives from several areas of concern, including the following.

1. At less than half of 1 percent (0.04 percent) of atmospheric gases, does CO_2 have the capacity to significantly affect global temperatures?

2. Does empirical data historically, even show that CO_2 affects temperature?

3. What is the integrity of supercomputer models to predict global warming?

A close examination of each of these areas would be needed.

CHAPTER XIV

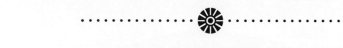

CO$_2$ Gas Controls Temperature— Reality or Fiction?

While CO$_2$ emissions are recognized as greenhouse gases, as already explained, they are minor, both in concentration levels and, arguably, their effectiveness as heat-trapping gases. The next charts Fig. 5. explain this further.

The following is an excerpt from the International Climate Science Coalition website, courtesy Jay Lehr, PhD. This is a public education piece and needs no further comment:

The above diagram of the gaseous content of Earth's atmosphere reveals in the lower right-hand corner the additional atmospheric carbon dioxide apparently resulting from all of the emissions of man's burning of fossil fuels over the last 200 years. These 200 years of emissions are represented by the one dot in the lower-right hand corner. This amount of man-made carbon dioxide equals 1/10,000 th of the gases comprising Earth's atmosphere. This miniscule amount of additional carbon dioxide is much too small to cause the catastrophes attributed to it such as dangerous climate change, melting glaciers, and threatening sea level rise.

Created for the public's education by Jay Lehr, PH.D.,

Fig. 5. Minuscule CO2 concentrations will have almost no effect on global warming

German climatologist professor Dr. Horst-Joachim Ludecke recently took data from two independent studies and superimposed them on a graph, appearing in *Nature* (2007). The first data set was global temperature anomaly going back 600 million years, taken from the results of a paper by Came and Veizer (*Nature* 2007, plotted in red). The second data set (purple) was for atmospheric CO_2 from a published study by Berner (*Nature* 2003). The plots were combined to see how well they correlated, if at all. Conclusion: no correlation!

For example, as the chart Fig. 6 shows, 150 million years ago, the atmospheric CO_2 concentration was over 2,000 ppm, and yet global temperature was more than 2°C below the long-term mean. Going back still further, the relationship is even more on its head .... CO_2 levels more than ten times today's level (415 ppm), yet the global temperature was a frigid 3.5°C below the mean.

Temperature vs CO₂
last 600 million years

Temperature data: Came and Veizer nature 449 (2007), CO₂ ; Berner Nature 426 (2003)

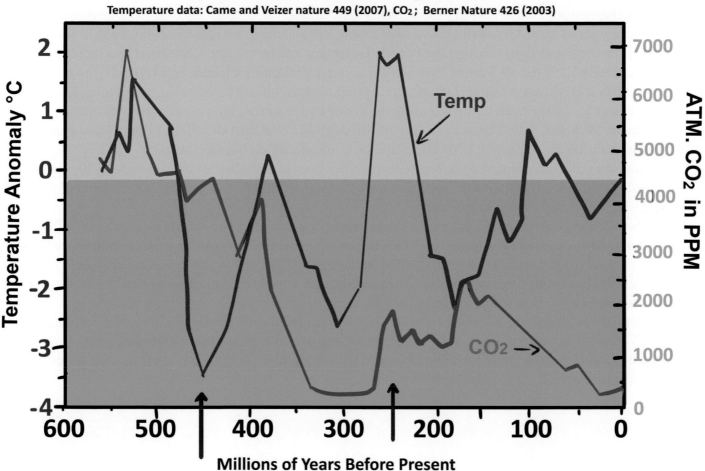

Fig. 6. No correlation between CO2 emissions and temperature

Most importantly, it should be noted that these long-term patterns tend to show CO_2 increases *after* temperature increases, not before. Perhaps more ominously, while temperature falls and rises randomly, CO_2 declines discontinuously but steadily. If that decline trend continues, the CO_2 will fall below what is essential for life on earth. At that point, all higher life dies.

We should be concerned with the present CO_2 levels at 415 ppm, not because they are "dangerously high," as the climate alarmists would have you believe, but because they are, in all probability, dangerously low! Maybe this mitigation strategy to further reduce CO_2 levels is taking us in the wrong direction.

CHAPTER XV

·············· ✻ ··············

If Not Carbon Factor, Then What?

The thermometer was in use in Europe by the early nineteenth century but only became common in America by about 1860. Gradually, it was used to monitor weather, and records showed a slow increase in temperature trend right through the twentieth century, and by the late 1990s, that had increased by approximately 1.7°F (or 1°C) from 1860. This was not a straight line trend, as it trended down in the 1970s with various sources (Time, Life, et cetera) predicting the onset of a new cold period (even ice age!). But this was to change back to the warming trend line by the 1980s. This modest growth rate reached its apex in 1998 and then began a leveling off through the first two decades of the present century (notwithstanding the strong El Niño effect in '14–'17, unrelated to climate change).

To restate this last point, the temperature trend has been essentially flat since the late 1990s (minus the ocean-warming effect known as El Niño, which is unrelated to climate change) in spite of ever-increasing CO_2 emissions in this period.

The following chart Fig. 7 highlights this trend based on actual data confirmation by weather balloons and satellite readings. Superimposed on this is the average of thirty-two model projections (red), which carry through to the end of the century. The mathematical algorithms driving this are based on as many as ninety assumptions, any one of which could cause a major deviation in the result. The outputs, therefore, are based on scientist assumptions, not science.

As might be expected, the end-of-century predictions from the various models vary considerably, from 5°F to 8°F (or approximately 2.5–4°C), measured over the preindustrial reference date (1860s). More noteworthy is the large deviation between the average of model projections (red) and the actual empirical data (blue).

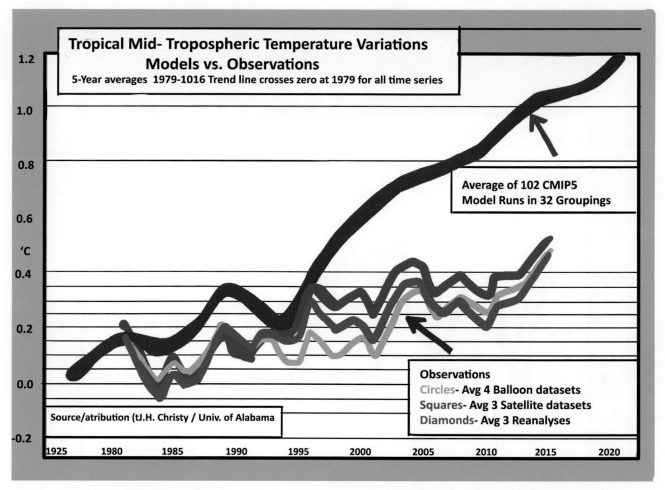

Fig. 7. Model shows temperature projections (red) not supported by actual empirical data (blue)

The UN IPCC has voiced only support for these conclusions with carefully worded qualifiers. But this is the basic analysis driving the so-called existential threat. It is a hypothesis with no sound data support, which, of course, is not science.

So back to the question, if not CO_2 and the vast post–World War II use of fossil fuels, then what is causing climate change and the phenomena of global warming?

All data points to the logical source—the sun. Solar activity combined with slight orbital changes has been responsible for the planetary temperature changes, as can be seen in the following chart Fig. 8. The temperature anomaly (blue) tracks the solar anomaly (red) very accurately, including the slight warming trend from the 1850s (1.7°F, 1.0°C) to 2000. Temperatures track solar, not CO_2, activity!

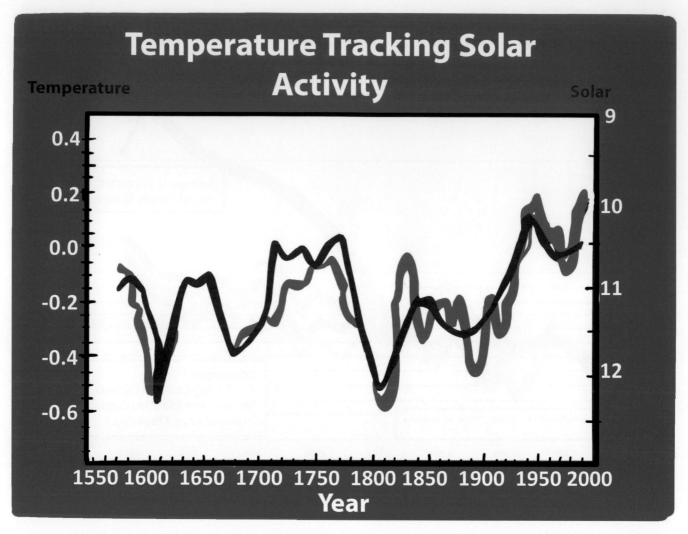

Fig. 8. The Sun and solar activity uniquely responsible for changes in temperature

But none of this empirical evidence appears to deter the climate activists. A major industry has grown around this alarmist movement. Worldwide, the climate change industry accounts for an estimated 500,000 direct employments, although many more thousands work in related industries, such as energy renewables. With livelihoods—and the funding that goes with the movement—on the line, this movement transcends any opportunity for questioning, let alone dialogue. It has all the characteristics of a religion, even a cult, replete with blind faith and rejection of nonbelievers. Because of its increasing influence and actual impacts on government policy, concern is growing about how this pressure is actually changing our way of life.

Modern civilization has made unprecedented progress over the last 150 years. Arguably, this progress has been made possible by abundant cheap energy, which fuels everything from electricity to transportation to plastics and synthetics. And more to the point, nearly 80 percent of this energy is, and will continue to be, delivered by fossil fuels.

It is estimated that there will be a phenomenal near 50 percent increase in the world economy from 2020 to 2040, caused by population increases (1.0 billion) and rising living standards in the third world. This is further estimated to trigger a 25 percent growth in just fossil fuel demand, in spite of pandemic and mitigation effects. Today's worldwide consumption of petroleum at 94 Mb/day will grow to 118 Mb/day.

With the oil industry being harassed, even intimidated, to transition to alternative energies, the question becomes, Where is this identified need for additional supply in the years ahead going to come from? Major oil companies, especially in green-obsessed Europe, have already announced cutbacks in capital budgets for exploration and new production, and this will have a significant impact on future supply. It is estimated that the industry requires over $500 billion in new capital investment to meet this need for additional oil and gas supply, and according to publicly stated plans, this is not happening.

What is happening is a shortfall that is already starting to affect supply and cause serious price increases. While private-sector oil companies are shrinking in importance, sovereign oil companies, headed by OPEC+, which includes Russia, are filling the gap and will continue to grow in importance. Our lost strategic opportunity will be new opportunity for these less-than-friendly suppliers!

Not that many years ago, OPEC instigated shortages, disrupted supplies, and caused prices to spiral upward in the whole Western world. A report from the authoritative *Wall Street Journal* adds a further interesting perspective:

> The UK and EU have pledged net-zero greenhouse gas emissions by 2050, closing coal plants and pouring billions into solar and wind projects. Germany and several other European countries have largely banned fracking. This has transformed European leaders into the equivalent of sixteenth-century naval explorers, praying for favorable winds and weather as energy prices rise and fall depending on cloud cover and wind conditions. Europe's willingness to harm itself in the name of unachievable climate goals is one of the greatest acts of democratic self-sabotage in history!

The forgoing scenario was not new, and the evidence had been accumulating for some time now; this was well known to APEX management. The only quasi mystery was how this climate change mania, backed only by bad science, was able to derail our modern economy, not to mention our industry. But just maybe a course correction is yet possible before it is too late.

Our presentation to the APEX Excom would have to outline these challenges. We could not talk to climate change issues without addressing these concerns. Above all, our focus would be on strategic opportunity for APEXEnergy.

CHAPTER XVI

······· ✸ ·······

Organization and the Fast Track

Our study work was winding down and reaching the finish line when one day, I was interrupted by a call to go to Jim Lavignon's office.

"Hey, Scott, shut the door. There's some pretty confidential stuff I want to tell you about. I just got out of a meeting with Jim Anderson and human resources that after several months of consideration, APEXEnergy has decided to establish a new department of environmental affairs and alternative energies. It will no longer be part of public affairs and will be a board-level department on its own and headed by a corporate VP, reporting directly to Mr. Anderson. Details are still being finalized, but I have been authorized to let you know that I will be raised to the VP level as head of this new department, and you, young man, will become general manager in charge of strategic development. So congratulations!

"The board has concluded that with the heavy shift to climate change and new energy technologies, APEX needs the organizational structure to address these challenges. Also, it is important that our allies and critics alike see the high profile APEXEnergy gives to environmentalism. More details on this reorganization will be announced at a later date. Meanwhile, we have been instructed to keep this confidential, and I know I can count on you to do so."

I, of course, congratulated him, and thanked him for his personal support of me in all of this. Then as I headed back to my office, I was left alone with my own thoughts.

Obviously, I felt a deep sense of elation. Early career success, recognition—it couldn't get any better! I had heard this term *fast track*, and I guessed I was on it! Further, I had the sense, not that I needed it, of even more commitment to this company, which had just shown such confidence in me.

In a broader sense, this was a good move by corporate because the world was changing fast and this would position us to respond with the necessary resources. Environment, and the inevitable slow transition to new technologies, would get the important attention we needed.

Also, I had to wonder how much these changes were motivated by pressure from the APEXEnergy maverick shareholders who were pushing for changes from the traditional fossil fuel business. They were clamoring for new thinking and even seats on the board to accomplish this. And all of that was building just weeks before our annual shareholder meeting? A well-timed announcement on all of this could help quash some of this mayhem from outsiders before that meeting. Whatever … from purely a good-business standpoint, these changes made a lot of sense.

But then, I had to make a call to a special someone in London.

"Hey, beautiful. Guess who?"

"Scott, my favorite climate activist! I haven't talked to you in forty-eight hours! That doesn't work anymore!" And then that infectious, deep-throated laugh.

"Eve, I have some big news … We have had a reorganization, and I have been promoted."

Her high-decibel "Congratulations" said it all!

Then she wanted to know how the big presentation was progressing. Again her ever present interest in the rather mundane subject of climate change never failed to fascinate and she didn't disappoint when she intervened, "Make sure you tell them that there is a large silent majority here in the UK who are not buying all this man-made global warming nonsense. Do you know that our electricity bills have increased more than threefold and it isn't even reliable? This Johnson government is going to have some real pushback at the next election. The silent majority will be silent no more! But there I go again when this is your big moment. Forgive me!"

"Only apologies in person accepted," I replied.

"Oh, naughty me. I forgot to tell you that I had already booked a flight to Houston a week ago. I guess it is another 'forgive me' moment!"

"Eve, my love, you are going to really like Texas!"

CHAPTER XVII

* * * * * * * * * * * ❋ * * * * * * * * * * *

Closing the Circle

We were now at an important juncture in our team's preparation. We had conducted a careful review of all available sources, and we agreed that that we had arrived at a fair assessment of the science behind climate change. Prior to our Excom presentation next week, we would need to provide an executive summary of major study points and our conclusions to the Excom members. This would provide the necessary background for our recommended actions at that meeting.

Our study team had concluded the following.

1. The body of scientific evidence on climate change does *not* support activist claims that carbon emissions are the cause of global warming. Therefore, the premise that we can control the earth's temperature through mitigation of emissions is inaccurate.
2. The world's main source of energy will continue to be fossil fuels well into the future. Efforts underway to suppress the industry that delivers this requirement, in favor of alternatives such as wind and solar, are misguided and will only reduce supply and cause higher prices for all petroleum products.
3. Private-sector major oil companies will continue to downsize in traditional oil and gas as environmental activism, backed in many cases by governments, promotes alternative energies. Meanwhile, sovereign oil companies, led by OPEC, will increase share and control of petroleum markets.
4. Renewable energy sources, including wind and solar, will continue to grow in importance but will also continue to be plagued by unreliability and high cost. Look to systemic energy supply disruptions in these sectors.

These conclusions, while not presenting a positive picture for an energy-hungry world, did frame the energy realities that faced us. APEXEnergy's challenge now would be to confront these realities in the most advantageous way to benefit the company's stakeholders. That meant devising an optimal strategy that would recognize not only climate change but also our already-significant commitment in developing new technologies. Though emission mitigation was misguided as a temperature control, the world was moving that way, and our shareholders would expect some compliance. This would not require that we abandon, or even diminish, our presence in the hydrocarbon business. Indeed, one of our main conclusions was that significant potential for growth existed in this industry and APEX's strategy should be to exploit this opportunity.

I had already been designated to make the final presentation to the Excom. The statement of our overall conclusions would provide the proper context for our final recommendations.

In the days ahead, we completed and submitted the executive summary according to plan. We received no immediate feedback, so I assumed the recipients were waiting for the final presentation.

Thursday, August 13, finally arrived, and Jim Lavignon and I, with the eight Excom members, assembled, awaiting Jim Anderson, our CEO.

The oak-paneled conference room was magnificent, right down to the furnishings and dark hues. It seemed like a quiet testimony to the importance of this major corporation, which spanned world commerce. And there I was, about to make a key presentation that would have important ramifications for the company's future. A little daunted, I surprisingly felt a quiet confidence. I knew my subject.

The subdued conversations going on around the conference table were suddenly interrupted with the entrance of Anderson, who, with a smile and a greeting, motioned to Lavignon that he could begin. After a few introductory remarks, Jim turned to me and said, "Scott, it's all yours."

"Gentlemen, good afternoon, and I hope you have had the chance to go over the summary of our climate change study sent to you in recent days. In the interest of brevity, we did not include a lot of detail, of course, but only highlights and conclusions that we felt would be of most interest to APEXEnergy. My purpose here today is to further summarize those conclusions and provide some recommendations. To that, my presentation chart summarizes our main recommendations with some supporting explanations, and of course, I will try to answer any questions you might have."

Climate Change Study Group's Major Recommendations

1. **APEXEnergy should officially come out in recognition of climate change.**

"This is an uncontroversial position because it is a simple scientific fact, and being clear and unequivocal about it confirms our good corporate citizenship. We believe in climate change, and of course, it has always existed on planet Earth, so we would be just emphasizing the obvious. APEXEnergy already takes this position, but we should emphasize this more."

2. **What should APEXEnergy's stance be on anthropogenic or man-made global warming?**

"This is a much tougher, even controversial question, yet this is the essence of the public outcry against the oil industry, and it must be addressed.

"It is a fact that CO_2 is a greenhouse gas and does have some reflection effect from the sun, though minor. One industry analysis concludes that if the most extreme model projections are correct, the effect on global temperatures would be miniscule (1/100th to 1/200th of a degree Fahrenheit by the end of the century), so technically, we can say yes, there is anthropogenic global warming, however small it may be. And we would be in line with our competitors—the Shells, BPs, and even Exxon—and hopefully be in agreement with our shareholders and customers.

"Our recommendation would be a principled yes! Though it is a fine line, we do meet the honesty and integrity test and avoid extremes of controversy."

"Mr. Paladino, excuse me for interrupting"—it was Gustavo Arroyo, senior vice president of Marketing—"but to your point that, yes, we should acknowledge man-made global warming, I hear your explanation. But does that not still contradict the actual science presented by your own analysis?"

My quick thought: Leave it to an engineer, and a PhD from MIT at that, to come up with that question.

"Yes, Dr. Arroyo, and we did have to examine this position long and hard before making this decision. And let me be clear: the fact that Exxon, an industry leader, seems to have already taken this position was not a factor. It is a fine line, but at the margin, it is technically correct: CO_2 is a greenhouse gas and does reflect, however minor, some sun off the earth's surface, which causes warming. To deny this is, in our opinion, a controversy not worth having.

"I think the real issue here is that the tremendous societal and economic costs being directed at this mitigation effort, in the end, result in no measurable result on temperatures. Temperature levels at century's end will be the same except for the cyclical, unalterable effects of natural climate change."

"Fair enough, Scott, but the fine line is pretty sensitive. Are there not some authoritative voices out there that speak to this? I would think messaging from the scientific community might resonate with the public better than an oil company that has a vested interest."

I answered, "There are those people out there, and many have spoken up, but in this politically charged environment, they tend to be dismissed as misguided skeptics or, worse, deniers. Let me cite an example of this: in recent public comments, a Canadian climatologist, formerly with Enviro Canada, stated that mean temperature patterns over South America and Australia are getting much colder than normal. This same expert states that, in contrast to global warming, the sun is entering a phase called *solar grand minimum*, which means we are heading for a colder climate in the next ten to twenty years.

"Pretty alarming news, and probably none of you have heard it before, in good part because it does not fit the narrative of the so-called existential threat due to global warming. Whether it proves to be true or not, it is scientific hypothesis, and like all science, should be questioned.

"So the answer to your question is that there is considerable pushback from well-placed sources even in academia, but the messaging to the public is being frustrated by a combination of government policy, special interests, and an ever-pliant media. Unfortunately, this is not just a passing trend but has become almost part of our culture.

"I will move on with our presentation."

3. **APEXEnergy has a good history of mitigating and reducing our carbon footprint.**

"We have invested over $1 billion to date in everything from smog reduction to water cleanup, methane and carbon capture and sequestration, right down to energy efficiency in our office buildings. That is a positive story that should be told.

"Our advertising agency has been instructed to develop some creative ideas to further promote this good corporate citizen image."

4. **APEXEnergy is researching new alternative forms of energy.**

"This has long been a major area of research and development in our AR&E labs. A basic tenet of the division mission statement holds that APEXEnergy will be an industry leader on new technology for energy transition.

"R&D projects have been underway for several years. A joint development project on new battery technology with a major car manufacturer will be announced soon. Also, a joint venture has been underway with Danish Wind Alternate Energy Inc. to develop high-strength plastic composites for large rotor blades used in wind farms.

"These new leading-edge technology initiatives we are pushing should be communicated to the public."

5. **APEXEnergy could take advantage of an opportunity now.**

"Although beyond the scope of this task force's mission, we thought it important to recommend that APEXEnergy consider taking advantage of a strong and increasing market demand for petroleum products, combined with a withdrawal strategy by our major competitors, and take the opposite strategy and go after this market.

"I would like to break out this important point a little further. With the help of our planning department, we have prepared the following chart Fig. 9, which highlights the world dependence on energy from basically all sources, both at present and into the 2040 time frame.

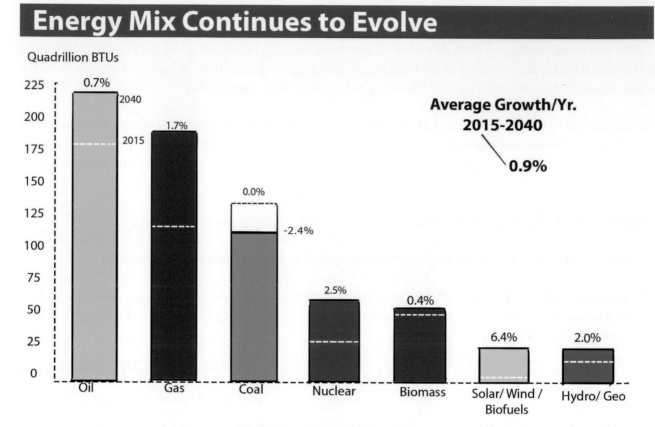

Fig. 9. World energy demand still dominated by fossil fuels well into mid-twenty first century.

"As you can see, oil and natural gas continue to grow while coal use shrinks, although it will still satisfy just under 18 percent of world energy because of growth in China and other non-OECD countries. Renewables—including solar, wind, and biofuels—are expected to show significant percentage growth from a relatively small base in 2020, but will still be a minor source for world energy, at less than 7 percent of the total, into midcentury.

"It is notable that these forecasts also project nearly 25 percent growth in the overall baseload demand for energy, and nearly 80 percent of that total will continue to be provided by fossil fuels. So in spite of major efforts to mitigate and reduce our carbon footprint through rationalization of petroleum use, it appears the world will be dependent on oil and natural gas well into the future. Though the percentage at 78 percent is slightly lower, the absolute amount is much higher. The question becomes, *Who is going to supply this demand?*

"Private-sector companies seem to be in retreat. Several well-known brands have already announced plans to cut back on their traditional business in favor of transitioning to alternative energies. That leaves this still-growing market basically in the hands of sovereign oil companies, such as OPEC+ which includes Russia. This does not have to happen. Gentlemen, we should take advantage of this business opportunity. We can exploit this opening in our traditional business, even as we maintain a leadership position in developing new energy alternatives."

I could see there was a lot of interest in the chart.

One question was raised: "Where is the actual evidence of the industry shifting away from oil and gas?"

I pointed out the publicly stated plans, especially in Europe, where Shell, BP, and Total had announced plans to de-emphasize their fossil fuel business and focus more on transitioning to alternative energies. "As a matter of record, capital budgets by oil majors are being cut back, and needed investment for new gas and oil development is being seriously compromised. The industry needs over $500 billion in new investment, and under present plans, that is not happening. This will only serve to transfer needed oil supply to OPEC and Russia with spiraling higher prices."

The head of APEX Energy Research and Engineering, and a gentleman I had met previously during my training orientation, then asked, "Scott, just looking at the chart, it would seem to me that your assessment for renewables is pessimistic. I have read reports as high as 25–30 percent in Europe and nearly the same for the U.S. by midcentury. How does that square with your numbers?"

"Your point is very valid. Certainly, the OECD countries of the developed world will have a more rapid transition, although our numbers indicate 17–18 percent in the U.S.–Europe area by 2040. The developing world, primarily in Asia and Africa, will transition much more slowly, and overall, our estimate is just short of 7 percent of world energy by 2040. There is no question that this sector is being propelled forward by broad government policy, including financing and tax subsidies. But as we assess the immediate future, questions of the overall efficiency and reliability of these systems still remain to be resolved. So far, these issues in North America and Europe have meant just lack of reliability and higher costs. The blackouts and brownouts in California and Texas and power disruptions and high electric rates in Europe are just a microcosm of some of the problems still plaguing that industry."

"These closing remarks cannot be described as a profile in optimism, but I think they reflect the reality of the world we live in. The world of energy is evolving, but as we have laid out, there is a clear opportunity to be had—if we choose to embrace it!"

There were some follow-up questions, which I was able to handle, and finally, Anderson broke in and said that our presentation seemed to cover most of the issues. The recommendations would be duly considered.

The meeting was adjourned. Any further follow-up could be pursued later.

As we left the conference room and headed for the elevator, a voice from behind me said, "Oh, Mr. Paladino, good presentation. Well done." It was Jim Anderson.

"Thank you, sir," I replied.

But then I was in a hurry to get to Houston International Airport. Eve Marie was arriving on the 5:45 British Air flight from London!

EPILOGUE

This short story outlines the journey of our protagonist, Scott Paladino, into the world of global warming and climate change in general.

Of course, he and the major oil company that he goes to work for are fictional. At the same time, many of the situations he encounters are based on actual events, and certainly, the hard science and empirical data that he discovers on the subject of climate change are not.

As a trained engineer in the environmental sciences, he evolves his thinking with serious questioning of the so-called science and the motives of the climate activist movement. After a deep dive into the actual science, he discovers that the much-maligned CO_2 emissions, increasing though they are, do *not* drive temperature increases. Solar variability is uniquely responsible. It is no mystery, then, that the climate models that predict extreme temperature increases to the end of this century have been, and continue to be, notoriously wrong.

Finally, it is worth noting many scientists and experts question or even reject the climate change movement. Ian Plimer, emeritus professor of earth sciences at the University of Melbourne, Australia, is one such critic. And he is quoted as saying, "Much climate 'science' is political ideology dressed up as science. There are times in history when the popular consensus is demonstrably wrong and we live in such a time. Cheap energy is fundamental for employment, for living in the modern world, and for bringing the third world out of poverty."

Printed in the United States
by Baker & Taylor Publisher Services